Copyright © 2018 Clavis Publishing Inc., New York

Originally published as *Het grote verstoppertjesboek van Piep* in Belgium and Holland by Clavis Uitgeverij, Hasselt–Amsterdam, 2016
English translation from the Dutch by Clavis Publishing Inc., New York

Visit us on the Web at www.clavisbooks.com.

Pip's Big Hide-and-Seek Book written and illustrated by Thaïs Vanderheyden

ISBN 978-1-60537-368-3

This book was printed in March 2018 at DENONA d.o.o., Zagreb, Marina Getaldica 1, Croatia.

First Edition
10 9 8 7 6 5 4 3 2 1

Clavis Publishing supports the First Amendment and celebrates the right to read.

PIP'S BIG
HIDE-AND-SEEK BOOK

Thaïs Vanderheyden

Clavis

NEW YORK

Do you see that little mouse by the tree over there?
That's Pip. He's playing hide-and-seek
with his mouse friends.
All one hundred of them!

Pip is counting.

1, 2, 3 . . . Come on, little friends; run as fast as you can!

4, 5, 6 . . . Quick, go hide in Mouseland!

7, 8, 9 . . . Oops, one little mouse fell down, see?

10 . . . Ready or not, here I come!

Ten little mice are hiding in the **circus caravan**. They are doing crazy things! Do you see the mouse in the elephant shower? And who wants a piece of cake?

The goldfish can do circus tricks too!
Look!

Far away in outer space, ten mouse friends are hiding in a spaceship! Can Pip find them all? What about you? Take a closer look in the cockpit!

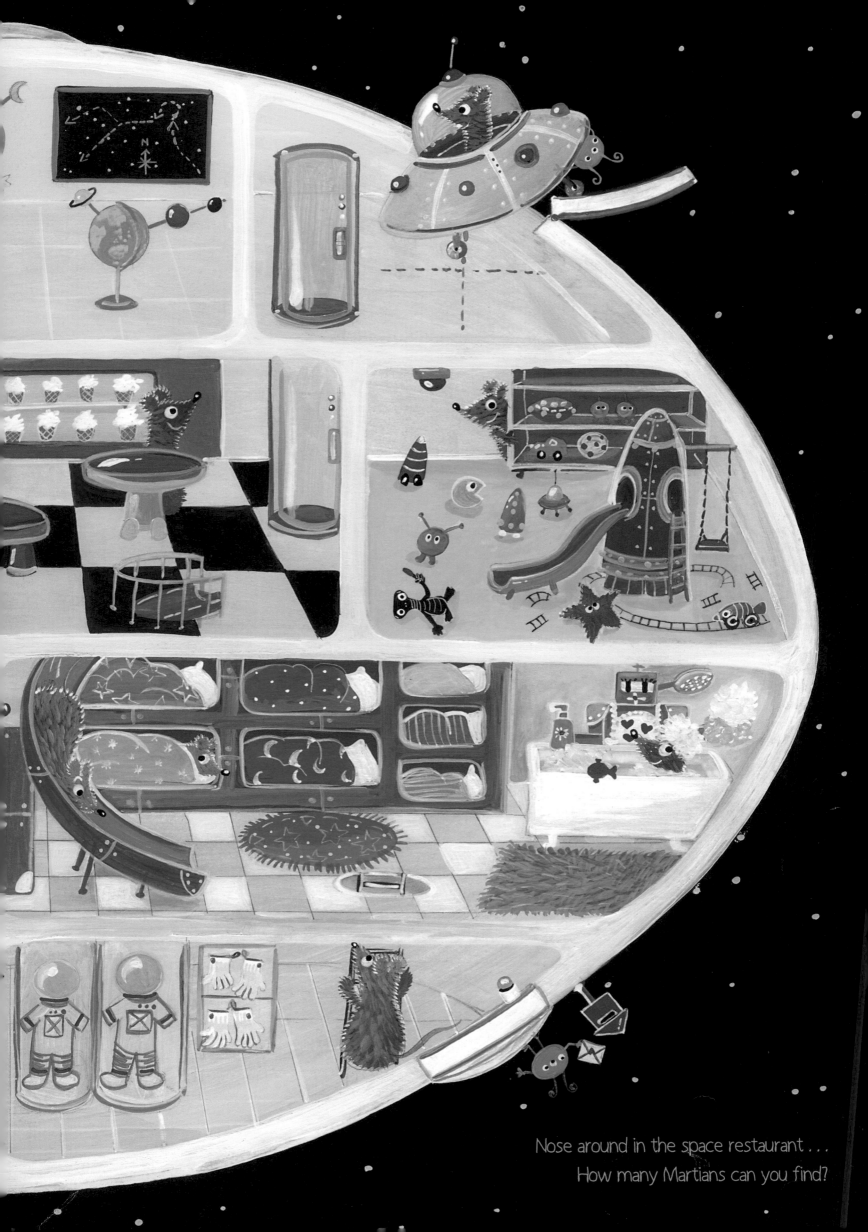

Nose around in the space restaurant . . .
How many Martians can you find?

High up in the old beech tree
there's an old **mouse hotel**.
Ten of Pip's little mice buddies
are hiding there!

Is one of them in the kitchen? No?
What about the dining room?
Or the sauna? And which mouse is
about to get a nice massage?

Shhhhh,
Mommy dragon is looking after her little dragon babies! Can you help Pip find the ten little mice hidden in the **mouse castle?**

Maybe there's one among
the crocodiles in the moat?
Will you help Pip find the treasure
in the castle too?

Take a deep breath and then . . . Splash! . . . Pip is looking for the next ten mice in a **submarine** underwater. Can you see them? Look in the cockpit. Or in the swimming pool. And what is on the menu in the canteen today?

Ten little mice are hiding in the **farm factory** deep under the ground. They're squeezed in between cheese, cake, and knitted caps.

Sugar

Which mouse is about to get an egg on his head? And who really needed to go to the bathroom?

-MENU-
- CAKE 1,
- CHEESE 1,
- TEA 1,

Pip is looking for the next ten mice high up in the sky ...in the **mouse blimp!**

Maybe there is a mouse under a blanket?

Is there a mouse in the bathtub?

And how many birds do you count in the cages?

Ten mice are hiding in the
surf shack on the beach.
Pip is looking in between the surfboards
and the coconut drinks.

Can you find the little mouse who's fishing for dinner? And which little mouse friend is hiding in the canoe?
What other animals do you see?

Coconut Bar

Phew, it's hot! Ten little mice are hiding
in the desert house. Pip is searching
in between the beautiful carpets
and in the bath!

Can you find all his mice friends?
And how many snakes do you count?

Brrr, it's so cold! Pip is looking for ten fluffy little mice in the **mouse igloo!** Maybe he finds one under the table? Or near the fireplace? And can you spot the piggy bank?

Hurray!
You helped Pip find all **one hundred** hiding mice!
It was such a fun **hide-and-seek adventure** ...
Pip is buying all his friends
ice cream and cotton candy!

Shall we play again? Who wants to count to **ten**?